I0566970

Epidemic 7.3k

Part One, Volume 1

Dean Hamid

Published by Dean Hamid LLC, 2022.

EPIDEMIC 7.3k
By
Dean Hamid

KALENE

January 9, 2032

The sounds in the darkness of the night would come and go. Sometimes loud, but many times not as loud at all. For sure, they were never quiet. Never. The screaming, shrill like sounds that would almost chill the insides of your soul, if that was any more possible than it was anyway.

The nights were bad. Real bad. Whenever we needed to move, it would always have to be during the day. At sun up. Approximately.

We never saw it coming. One day, we were just getting reports that it was a virus with flu-like symptoms. It started in the Midwest and soon escalated quickly to the East Coast. Of course, measures were taken, but it was never considered serious. Even the Government wasn't too hard on it. Yeah, wash your hands and stuff like that but, for the most part, it didn't command any more respect than the common cold.

But, then, one day it just happened. People started dying. By the hundreds. Then, the thousands. It quickly spread throughout the nation and, soon afterward, a panic ensued. The Government tried to calm everyone down, but it was to no avail. Right afterward. Like days afterward, something horrible happened.

The people who died as a result of the virus started coming back to life. The corpses wouldn't stay dead. They were literally clawing their way out of the ground. Walking among the living.

Some thought it was a miracle. Something Biblical. The second coming or something. They even welcomed them into their churches, synagogues and, some, even their homes.

Then, it turned ugly real quick. The dead would seem to sleep during the day but, at night, it was different, everywhere. They would want to eat. People even tried to feed them, but the food they fed them wouldn't stay down until, one day, one of them took a bite off the living and it was then that all hell broke loose.

Pandemonium spread quickly among the country. They were eating people indiscriminately. And, what made it worse was that they could not be killed. Hell, after all, they were already dead.

We, my mom and brother, lived in a neighborhood located on the South side of Chicago. A place called Lincoln Park. Even before the epidemic got worse, we were plagued by gang violence in our neighborhoods. Children were getting killed indiscriminately by stray bullets. Violence between gang rivalries erupted in the streets all the time. People were killed, sometimes in their own homes as they slept.

As bad as that was, this was worse. Some of those same members of those same gangs were now the walking dead. And, even worse, they were now side by side with their unfortunate victims hunting down and feeding on the living.

Me and my family and some others stayed downstairs, hunkered down in the basement of the Tribune Tower building. Safe. For now. The windows were blocked and sealed up on boards. Men with guns patrolled frequently at night, keeping an eye out. Food was gathered throughout the day.

Even that became dangerous, the gathering of food. Some of the food itself had become infected. And, then, the people that became infected started hunkering down in those same stores. Like they were waiting. Setting traps. It was difficult and very dangerous, making your way in without being attacked.

There were also battles between other survivors for food. Food was scarce and short all over. People were being killed, not only by the undead but the living as well. Many resorted to living like savages, attacking others in droves.

I started this journal just in case I didn't make it. So, that someone would find it in case I don't make it out of this alive. I mean, I'm not scared. I just want someone to know what happened because I'm afraid there aren't going to be too many left at the pace this is going.

I figured if I secured it at the Harold Washington Library it would be safe there at least. There's nothing to eat there. Just quietness. Darkness. And, a lot of books. I spend a lot of my time there. Reading. It's been my sanctuary of sorts.

But, on the way there, one morning with my brother, we were attacked. We fought the creatures off as hard as we could. Finally, we broke free and made it back to the shelter. We told no one about it because we weren't supposed to have left by ourselves anyway. Unfortunately though, I noticed, a few days later, a sore on my brother's arm started to spread. He'd been bitten.

We'd have to leave soon or I feared he would become like the undead. So, I am leaving this journal behind. A record, in hope that whoever finds it may know the truth of what happened to us. To my family. To my world.

I'd have to leave it somewhere. Somewhere where, hopefully, someone would find it. This epidemic can't last forever, I hope. Humanity will have to live again. That's the resilience of the human being. But, where?

Of course. The library. Amongst all the literature. Someone would have to find it. I'll leave later on tonight. And, subsequently, forever. I'll sneak out before sunrise. Take a candle, so I can see. Be careful, the atmosphere there is literally bone dry and just one spark could set off a flame. I'd never forgive myself if I set fire to the place.

CHICAGO TRIBUNE
January 10, 2032
Virus under control. Thousands Worldwide saved.
Scientists have found a cure. They're calling it 7.3000. Because of the onslaught, prolonged testing will not happen. The President has agreed, along with other World leaders, that this cure should work to actually paralyze the undead creatures long enough for them to be destroyed.

Scholars are afraid that humanity will never know its past or exactly whatever happened to start this awful outbreak. And, more so, how this untested cure that they created can further stop the onslaught of mankind.

It didn't. In fact, it got worse.

JAMEL / KEVIN

February 15, 2033

It's getting harder and harder to find food. Supplies. Anything. The stores are wiped out and it's becoming more dangerous now to even walk the streets, much less go inside a store. The last place we got supplies was at the Mall, and making our way out of that hell hole cost us supplies.

These creatures seem to be setting up traps. How can something be dead? Something that can't even think, set up traps. Stalk its prey? They're doing it though. And, they're getting better at it.

Ever since the so-called great cure, when people came back out thinking it was safe again. The cure that the so-called scientists told us had killed off the virus. People finally came out of hiding. Walking around these creatures who were presumably dead.

Then, suddenly, they came alive. Just like that. The massacres were unbelievable. People were being killed in droves. Children. The elderly. All killed. They invaded hospitals that many had gone to for treatment. For help. They attacked these places and slaughtered people by the scores.

The ones who escaped made their way back into hiding. But, it wasn't safe anymore. Those who came out of hiding and were infected came back to those same places and slaughtered them like cattle.

Panic ensued right afterward. The Military. At least what was left of the Military opened up its bunkers to the remnants of the remaining survivors. Places that were hidden for decades. Some even centuries. Secret underground warehouses. Places that were now homes to the survivors of this hellified holocaust. But, they only did it for the select. People who had money. Like, what good was money now? But, they turned the ones who didn't have any away.

Me and my homies stayed in the Bronx, in the projects. A place called Edenwald. Many of us held out there for a long time, staying protected by the code of the streets that we lived by. We kept watch and looked out from on top of the buildings. Keeping the doors secured in these brick and mortar concrete ghettos that New York City once called dilapidated, but was now considered safe havens, citywide.

Oh yeah, there were some that tried to infiltrate. Some that even tried to disguise themselves as decrepit. The same ones that looked down on us. That treated us like shit. They literally came begging. Many were turned anyway, but some weren't. Others were even used as sacrifices. Letting the infected feed on them until they get their fill and subsequently leaving us alone until the next time.

What a hell of a way to exist. But, we were existing, and that was good enough, for now. Still don't know what started this virus. Don't know about no cure. Nothing. All we concentrate on is living day to day. Surviving. Hell of a way to live for cats like us, like myself, my homie Jamal, but it was living.

ED

Ed didn't know what started this whole thing, and he really didn't give a damn. He was just about his business, and that was survival. When the virus came and the Governor locked the city down, he knew shit was about to go bad quickly.

At first, most folks stayed calm and started doing whatever they, they being the Government, asked them to do. But, after a while, things went sideways.

People started dying. And, then, those things; they just wouldn't stay dead. As crazy as it was, most people called it a miracle. The government laid claim to it, of course. Said they discovered a cure. A way for people to live forever. It sounded good. Real good.

But, for those people like Ed. People that lived in the inner-city. It didn't last long. Hell. Not only did they not die. They also didn't sleep. At first, their skin stayed right, healthy, at least until all the blood ran out of their body. Then, the flesh started falling off their bones. Their hearts weren't beating either. They were dead.

Then, out of nowhere, they started biting people. Nibbling at first, but not long afterwards if you were caught alone. They would attack you. Eating people. It was crazy. Then, you couldn't kill the bastards. You could shoot and shoot, but they kept coming at you. At first, the Police came to their aid. Then, the National Guard. Then...it was just people. Everyday people. Cooks. Bus drivers. Office workers. Just everyday people.

Ed was a Corrections Officer that worked on Rikers Island. He wasn't at work on the day when all the hell broke loose, but he wished he had. Being that it was an Island, they stayed safe for a while. Locked it down. But, all it took was one. One person. That person turned into a creature. Started biting everyone. Staff. Inmates. The next thing you know, people were swimming across to LaGuardia Airport trying to escape. Some had even made it. The ones that didn't drown were infected.

Right afterward, it spread across the city like wildfire. The cops panicked. Hell, there was an ass of looting everywhere. Stealing. They couldn't be everywhere. When they did send the National Guard in, they started shooting at people indiscriminately. Everything that moved. That's when they found out that the infected couldn't die. They quickly left, and the city had to fend for itself.

That's why guys like Ed became assets. They had guns. They were trained to protect. And many were Civil Service workers that lived in the inner city. They, in a sense, became the Police. The Court Officers. School Safety Officers. Any job that required a gun.

IT WAS JUST BEFORE sun up, and Ed was leading a crew to get some supplies from downtown Brooklyn. A few years earlier, Barclays Stadium was set up for a food bank of sorts. But, when those things, those creatures, caught wind of people coming that way, they set traps. Slaughtered hundreds. So, now you had to be very cautious. Very cautious indeed.

Ed had made this run many, many times before, but he still remained as cautious as if it was the first time. He'd been attacked once before and lost some people as a result of.

He crossed Flatbush Avenue from Ft. Green and looked back at his people. Jamal, Kevin, and Kalene. The only other one toting a gun was

Kalene. She was from Chicago. She'd made her way to New York after the first big cure wave in Chicago. Kevin and Jamal were gang bangers from the Bronx. They just kind of migrated to Brooklyn, at least that's what they said. Don't know what set they banged, Crip or Blood. At this point in the game, it really didn't matter. Ed just wanted and needed people with enough guts and balls to make these runs with him.

It would have just been another one of those days too. Another run, but something about it seemed off and Kalene noticed.

"Ed, something doesn't feel right."

"Kalene, just let it go. You're always trying to jinx something. Just let it go," Kevin said.

"No Kevin. For real. It's just too quiet."

"Come on Kalene with the bullshit-"

"Quiet," Ed said as he gave the sign to stop. "She's right. Something does seem a little off."

"What do you mean?" Jamal asked as he looked around.

"It's just too damn quiet."

"It's always quiet. Those things aren't out yet," Jamal said.

"But still. The birds. Anything. Stray dogs. Hell, they scavenge during the day as well too. But nothing." He pointed around them. "Do you hear... anything?"

"Yeah, yeah..." Jamal listened.

"Well. What do you want to do? Turn back around?" Kalene asked.

"Maybe we should-" Ed started to say.

"Fuck that! We've come this far. There's no food. We're running short as hell and no telling when we'll get another shot," Kevin spit.

Ed sighed. He knew he was right but, still, there was something that didn't sit right with him about it. "Ok. Let's go. Everyone, just be on point."

They crept closer towards downtown. They'd pinpointed Concord Market. Their target. Figured they'd go in and fill up on canned goods and hygiene before nightfall and get on through.

Ed pointed Kalene and Kevin inside. They carried duffel bags over their shoulders. Jamal stood point towards the entrance of the alleyway that ran towards the side into the back alleyway. Ed kept his eye out in front.

Kalene and Kevin made their way towards storage. It was ransacked, but there were still good selections of canned food, so they stuffed their bags. Remaining close to one another, they made it over to the utility section. Kevin snatched up some batteries and some wiring to repair some broken lighting, and nails to seal the boards on the windows and doors. Things that were needed to keep the building they lived in safe.

He turned towards Kalene, ready to go; then, he saw something move behind her. He pointed, and she turned around. Not seeing anything, they started back out the same way that they came in. Then, a few steps short of the entrance, out from the shadows, something or someone jumped out in front of them. A creature.

Kalene turned and fired a few rounds, and it only slowed it down some. She took aim again and fired a few rounds at its head and, finally, it went down. Ed rushed inside the building. "What the fuck! Come on! Hurry!"

Jamal came from around the corner hauling ass inside. "Ed, there's an ass of them! They're coming out the back of the building!"

Ed looked outside at the sky and said. "Why? It's still daylight."

"Something changed!" Kalene shouted. "We've got to get the hell out of here. We can't get trapped."

"She's right Ed."

"Alright. Kevin, you got to get rid of some stuff, so you can keep up! Kalene, you play the point. Me and Jamal will be right behind y'all, trying to keep them at bay."

"Which way!" Kalene looked around.

"Ft. Green side. Towards Myrtle Avenue. Straight up the avenue! There's some people I know down that way that will give us cover if needed."

Kevin heard them coming. The noise. The screeching. Peeping around the corner, he saw a few coming towards them, getting closer. "We've got to go now!" he yelled at them.

They ran out the building and Kalene led the way, running up DeKalb Avenue towards Ft. Green. Kevin was right behind her. They could hear the gunshots as Ed fired into the thong of creatures that chased behind them.

Flatbush Avenue and the distance between them widened, and they could see some fall behind. But, still, they kept it moving until they couldn't see any of them at all. It wasn't until they got to Fulton Street, about a few miles away, did they stop and rest.

"Is everyone alright?" Ed asked.

They all answered in the affirmative. They were all just winded.

Kevin looked behind them, then said, "What the hell was that about?"

"Yeah, I know. It's still daylight. I thought they didn't come out during the day, Ed," Jamal said.

Ed looked behind them as well, then solemnly said, "I did too."

"This is definitely a problem. Just like in Chicago," Kalene sighed.

CHICAGO

Kalene drifted back to Chicago. She couldn't get it out of her mind. Along with it came the headaches. Migraines. That day.

It was a little after 4 that morning, and Kalene woke up out of her sleep. It wasn't a nightmare this time, even though she'd had her fair share. Chicago stayed on her mind. Her family. Her friends. Her brother. Dead. Gone.

After her brother got bit, everything went south fast. Sure, the cure seemed to paralyze those creatures, the undead, for a while but, then they only rose back up with a vengeance. And also immune.

She took her brother to one of the shelters. She had to beg him to go. The wound started spreading. It didn't even scab. After much pressuring, he finally gave in.

She also told her mother what had happened. Of course, she was definitely disappointed that they'd left out that night, but she knew her son needed help immediately, so she packed up some bags for the trip.

Kalene led them all to Grady Park, where they had makeshift medical shelters set up for the infected by the Military. Her mother went in first because she gave the less threatening persona, and the guards were very tense.

Describing the incident that took place to them, at least what Kalene had told her, the doctors from the Government agreed to let Kalene's brother in, but only if they could use a new cure that they were developing on him. Her mother and brother had no choice, and neither did Kalene. Her brother seemed like he was getting worse daily. The bite looked infected. So, they agreed.

Once in, they were given shelter, food, and fresh clothing. They were also allowed to wash and get themselves cleaned up. The place was heavily fortified, so they were safe, and Kalene's brother seemed like he was getting better day by day. A few weeks had passed, and they all felt at ease. Kalene let her guards down. And, so did her mother and brother. The big mistake.

They woke up to screaming and the all too familiar shrills that they thought they'd left behind. Kalene woke up thinking it was just a dream, but it wasn't. Far from it. The smoke in the air and the screaming convinced her mind otherwise.

She looked over at her mother, and she too was awakened out of her sleep. Looking across from her, her brother's bed was empty. She glanced over at her mother, telling her to get dressed, but she was already on it. "Kalene. We have to find your brother!"

"But, Mom. What's happening!"

Her mother eased over towards the door and started peeping out. "I don't know, but I damn sure recognize those screams."

Kalene was right behind her. They eased the door open and looked out. Creatures were stalking the hall. Some were literally eating the doctors and scientists as they tried to get away. They shut the door back. "Mom, we've got to get the hell out of here!"

"Not without your brother!"

Kalene looked around the room for a weapon, and the best thing she could find was a broom. She rushed over, grabbed it, then broke it in half and gave the other half to her mother. "Here, if they get up on you. Jab this in their eye all the way into the brain."

Her mother nodded, yes. Kalene grabbed her knapsack and stuffed it with a few items, then ran back over to the door where her mother was. She leaned against it and started telling her. "Okay. We'll search around for Mark. Then, get the hell out of here."

"He might have gone to the vending machines. You know how he is about late night snacks and that medicine he was taking always made him hungry."

She was right. "Okay. We make it up the hall and to the left where they're at. We'll check the rooms nearby in case we don't see him. He might be hiding out."

"Okay."

They busted out the door and were immediately tackled by a creature. Kalene stabbed it in the eye, twisting it deeper, then she pulled it back out. She got up and pointed her mother towards the vending machines. She was blindsided by one as well, but she managed to turn from out of its grasp and then stabbed the jagged sharp broomstick into its eye.

They were confronted a few more times like that, and then Kalene pointed towards the vending machines up the hallway in front of them. He wasn't there. Her mother nodded; then, Kalene started looking inside the rooms, yelling out her brother's name. Nothing. They made it towards a few more rooms, and then they finally spotted him.

Eating on a body, it was her brother. He'd turned into a creature. She called out to him and, when he heard, he turned towards them. Kalene turned her face away in disgust. His face seemed like it was drained of blood; his skin chalky white and eyes were bloodshot red.

Her mother caught up to her and, when she saw him, called out his name. She started to approach him, but Kalene held her back saying, "Mommy, he's not the same."

"He's my son."

"No, he's not Mark. He's something... different."

She pulled away from her and ran towards him. Easing up to him, she put her hands out and moved closer. "It's me, Mark. Your mother. I've got you." She finally managed to sit next to him and started hugging him.

Kalene actually thought for a minute that maybe he was alright. Maybe he just needed some more medicine or something.

Her mother hugged him as she cried. "Baby, it's gonna be alright." She looked back at Kalene and said to her, "He probably just needs some more drugs or something. We need to get him to another shelter. We'll find another one."

Kalene looked around at the carnage and frowned. "But, mom, there's no one left. We're alone."

"Then, we'll go somewhere else. We found this place. There's got to be another." She started to plead their case. Mark stared up at her. Then, he looked at his mother. The tears that continued welling up in her eyes. He didn't get it though. They were now strangers to him.

Kalene thought maybe her mother was right. They could at least find a little more medicine in this place, then get Mark to another facility. Maybe, he wasn't that bad. But, those thoughts quickly withdrew from her mind when Mark turned towards his mother and bit her in the face. He continued biting, feeding on her, trying to get to her brain.

Kalene screamed for him to stop, but he didn't. It was no use, and it was like her mother didn't even struggle. Her son, her baby. But, to Kalene, her brother was no longer there. He was a creature. A monster who just attacked and killed their mother. She screamed and rushed towards him. Holding the jagged but sharp stick, she held it over her head and sunk it deep into his head and started twisting it. Blood and brain matter gushed out and oozed all over the ground, but she continued stabbing until he finally stopped moving.

She got up breathing heavily, looking over at her mother. Her brother. Her only family. What was she going to do now? She got her answer quickly. A bunch of other creatures had spotted her and charged towards her. She tried to grab at the stick and pull it out of his head, but it broke. She backed herself up against the wall. Scared. She screamed; she didn't know what else to do.

Glancing over at one of the waiting rooms, she looked over at the window, leading outside. It was wide. She started running towards it.

Maybe, she could get someone's attention. Some help. She looked out and didn't see anyone. Looking down, it was about a two-story drop.

The creatures chased after her. She tried to pry the window open, but her thoughts quickly changed after she turned and saw they were up on her. She backed up slightly then screamed, charging at the window. It shattered and she fell to the ground below, unscathed.

Looking up, she saw some other people backed up against the windows also. Some were fighting the creatures. Some were just being eaten alive. Some even looked at her and decided to do the same thing she did. Jump. But, they were much higher. It would mean death, but a much better death than they were facing.

But, the creatures figured they'd also do the same thing. Jump. They couldn't die, and so they did. Now, they were free. Kalene had to go. She had to leave. She ran as far as she could.

Hiding in garbage bins at night, she survived by eating from the garbage as well. She thought she wouldn't make it. That she would eventually be discovered. She thought about giving up more than once, until she ran into a bus filled with survivors and guns.

They checked her out first, making sure she wasn't bitten. When they found out she was okay, it was only then did they invite her into their shelter. They gave her food. Clothing. When they asked her where she wanted to be dropped off, she asked instead, where were they going? Probably set up another shelter in Chicago, one said. Then another said, let's try New York. I heard about ships going across the ocean into Africa. Some have even said the virus had died down quite a bit.

He'd convinced them and they agreed it was worth a shot, and Kalene was asked what she wanted to do. She didn't take long thinking about it. She answered, "New York."

So, that's how she caught up with the migration heading East. The plan was to make it to the shore. Catch a ship going to Europe or somewhere across the water. They'd heard that it was under control over there.

Lies. All lies. Shit was bad all over, if not worse in New York. She left the people she was with and sought shelter with another crew. A crew from Brooklyn. Ed's crew.

She ended up staying in Bed-Stuy. But, she'd frequently bounce back and forth to Bushwick Projects on a regular basis. Bushwick Projects buildings were tall. Twenty stories. Up top, you could see into Manhattan and across Brooklyn, damn near into Queens, and it was used as a headquarters of sorts. Letting people know exactly what was going on and where. At least, that was always the plan.

But, like everything else, people had to stick to the plan in order for it to work. And, most people did whatever the hell they wanted to do anyway. And on that side of town, Bed-Stuy, it was rob, steal, and loot. So, most of the time, Bushwick Projects served as a lookout as well, not from the creatures though but from the living. The thieves, killers, and even the rapists.

Bushwick Projects had guns, firepower. She didn't know why. She remembered Ed telling her why, and something to the effect of that's just how things sort of happened. Most of the major dope dealers started over that way, and they were heavily armed. When those creatures manifested themselves, they took flight. Left the people to fend for themselves. Left the dope and also the large cache of weapons they had stashed as well.

Ed and some people he knew, knew about the stashes and locked it down. Distributing the weapons and even the ammunition only as needed. Kalene would keep watch and Ed trusted her, along with a few others.

Finally, they made it back to Bushwick in one piece. She walked up to the rooftop where Ed hung out, looking over Manhattan. She crept up behind him, but not too silent so as to startle him.

"Hi Ed. It's pretty late for you to be up."

Ed turned towards her and said, "Same for you. Is everything alright?"

"Sure. Just couldn't sleep."

"Nightmares... again."

"No. Just restless." She walked over towards the edge and looked downtown. "That was some pretty weird shit earlier today."

"Crazy as hell, to say the least."

She turned towards him asking, "What do you think happened?"

"Happened?" His head turned towards her.

"Yeah. They came out during the day."

"Oh yeah. Definitely different. I was just thinking about that myself."

"Do you think they're adjusting?"

"To what? The sunlight?"

"Yeah."

"God. I hope not. But, we saw what it was with our own eyes."

Kalene walked over towards the other edge and stared out towards Manhattan. "Ed... we lost things hauling ass from them..."

Ed walked over towards her, sighed, then looked at her. Sighing again, he answered, "That was on my mind also. We've got to make another trip."

"There..." Kalene sighed as well pointing downtown, then also pointed towards Bed-Stuy. "Or, to the Armory because we're almost out of bullets."

"Damn." Ed emitted a long, deep audible breath expressing his sadness and, right now, tiredness as well. "Both."

The Reality...

Kevin spied the convenience store from off the corner of the building. It was abandoned, but it wasn't the people that he wanted. It's what he needed. He checked his gun, making sure the safety was off before he headed towards it.

Subsequently, the area was supposed to be safe, but things happened earlier. Ever since he made that run downtown with Ed and them, he'd heard reports that the creatures were making their way deep into Bushwick. Good reports from very reliable sources.

He didn't trust it though. But, the store had what he wanted. He needed a smoke. He had some loose tobacco he had salvaged from a smoke shop a couple of weeks back. Now, all he needed was some rolling paper.

He'd been in there before looking for cigarettes; of course, that was all gone, but he remembered the rolling papers. Now, he needed to make this move to get his long waiting "nic" off. A nice roll-up would be nice right about now, he figured.

He came out into the open, looking around. Seeing no one outside, he continued on towards the street. He made it across and hit the wall of the building in front of him, hugging it firmly with his back. He glanced up at the windows in the building he'd just left and saw a few people looking out at him. He caught someone's eye and they signaled him, telling him that the coast was clear. He signaled back his thanks.

He crept up the side of the street, ducking down very cautiously. He made it. He glanced quickly and looked through the smashed windows, looking for any movement. None. He slowly opened the door. He pointed his gun outward in front of him as he made his way in. He didn't have to go far. Just across the counter. He jumped over and started searching frantically amongst the trash that was scattered about. There. He spotted a pack. He reached down and that's when he heard the throat-gurgling shriek. The creature's signature scream.

He stayed down. Peeping his head up, he spotted it towards the back in the shadows. Kevin knew it wouldn't make a move towards the front because of the sunlight peering through, so he made his way back cautiously across the counter. It could still lunge at him, so he backed up very cautious-like. Then, off to the side, he was blindsided. One of them had come around from the back. He'd been set up. Tumbling to the ground, he dropped his gun. He tried scrambling to get it, but the creatures had grabbed hold of his legs, trying to drag him back into the shadows. Kevin fought for his left, kicking frantically.

He tried reaching for the gun, but it was useless. More creatures from the back came out and started helping. Kevin kicked, struggling as hard as he could and, just when one of them started to lunge at him, someone busted through the door. Jamal. He started shooting. Still, they wouldn't stop approaching. He reached for his machete and started chopping them across the head. Stunning them momentarily, but one screeched at him and started to charge. Kevin was finally able to grab his gun, and he turned and fired. He emptied the clip into its head.

The others moved back slightly after Jamal chopped him in the head again. It was done. Kevin jumped to his feet and they both grabbed each other and started backing out the door.

They were out of bullets, so they knew they would have to make a mad dash towards the building because they heard more, and it seemed like they were coming their way. More screeching and shrieking. Kevin glanced up and yelled out, "Damn, it's still daylight!"

"It doesn't matter to them anymore. Those muthafuckas done got immune or something."

"We've got to go!"

They were right. They both looked over towards Bushwick Avenue and a bunch had gathered looking their way. Spotting them, they started approaching fast. Kevin glanced back up at the window where he'd seen someone earlier, and they were waving her hands frantically. Pointing behind them. He looked. There were more. He grabbed at Jamal and pointed their way. "We've got to go."

Jamal wasted no time. They hauled ass across the street, but their way was blocked. A few of them had come from around the building where they just came from. Kevin pointed his gun and pulled the trigger. Nothing. He forgot he'd emptied the clip in the store. He didn't bring another one because he wasn't expecting any of this to happen.

They stood back to back now.

"Bruh. Just fight. Fight as hard as you can. Fuck it," Kevin said as he balled up his fist.

"Damn right. Fuck them."

They put up their hands and, when one of them lunged, he was popped in the head by a bullet. His head exploded. They shielded their eyes to prevent the infected splatter from getting in their eyes.

"Get the fuck down!" It was Ed. He aimed and another one dropped. The next one was up too close for him to unload. It was close up for him to swing. One swipe from the machete he brandished and the creature's head fell off. "C'mon on!" he hollered at them.

Jamal and Kevin started running, but Kevin stopped and, feeling through his pockets, he looked back on the ground where he'd come from. He'd dropped the rolling papers. Jamal looked back and screamed. "Are you fucking serious!"

He was.

He went back and picked them up and the creatures started chasing him. He made it around the corner with Ed, beckoning him to run faster. They were right on his ass. He dived through the door, and Ed quickly closed it up then put up the steel barricade. They all backed away slowly, looking at the creatures as they banged furiously, trying to get in. Before long, there were at least 20-30 more.

Things were changing now. The monsters could come out during the day. Ed knew they couldn't hold them off for long. A couple of tenants came down checking out the action, and they looked at Ed in distraught. They knew it too. It would only be a matter of time before they made it through the barricades. They had no choice, they had to leave. But, as Ed watched, he couldn't help but wonder, where to?

EVERYONE FROM THE BUILDING had gathered in the basement. Some had managed to make their way from the other neighboring buildings as well. As crowded as it was, still, caution was the rule. Men with rifles were placed by the windows. The doors were thoroughly secured.

Ed and some of the elders that had been through the ringer with him since the beginning of this epidemic stood behind him. A table was set up where those that represented the community sat. Ed signaled to a man standing over to the side and he started hollering out for everyone to be quiet.

It didn't take long or too much to quiet them down. He pointed towards the elders up front. A woman with long flowing gray hair stood up. She was petite for a woman of age, but her body appeared very strong. She was well respected because as soon as she started to speak, you could hear a pin drop. She said, "My people. My people. As you know, it's been a hard ten years. Ten years it's been this epidemic. But, for some of us, it was hard even before then." The crowd nodded their heads in agreement.

But, even now. As soon as we get adjusted... well," she sighed, "as adjusted as we can." She'd lost many family members. She pulled herself together and said at the top of her voice. At least as loud as it would go. "These creatures are changing. Before we had them on the run, but now… now, something else has happened…" Her voice trailed off and then another man stood up.

"Thank you, Mama Eva." He motioned for two younger men to escort her to a cushioned seat behind them. He started to survey the crowd, then said, "Yes. Things changed, but we had the feeling it would come to this." He pointed to the windows. "It's daylight and these… things, roam the streets now. Making it damn near impossible and definitely unsafe to even be out."

"Well! What the hell do we do?" a woman screamed out from the crowd.

"Yeah. What the hell are we going to do now!" another hollered out.

That started a plethora of shouting and unrest among them. The woman who spoke earlier tried to quiet them down, but it wasn't working. Ed got up on top of a table and hollered out, "Quiet down! Just shut up for a couple minutes. All this screaming and panicking won't get us nowhere!"

"You say that, but you carry a gun. You're safe!"

"And I've put my gun and my life on the line to help each and every one of y'all. So, right now, I deserve your respect! And I need you to listen!"

The crowd silenced and their attention was directed towards him.

"Now. Apparently, we don't have enough guns for everyone. We'd catch pure hell trying to shoot them all anyway. But, we have to be able to move around. To get food. Right now, this is the best shelter we've got. They can't get in, so far. From atop the building, we can contact other people to know where the food and resources are. We at least have that on our side."

"So, what you're saying is we're trapped," someone said.

"It could be worse."

"My cousin was telling me about a place. A safe place. Protected by the Military."

Ed had heard about this as well. The place was Roosevelt Island in the city. It was supposed to be safe. Granted, it was surrounded by water and all, but he knew from when he was on Rikers Island how dangerous that could be. If someone got sick, they'd' catch hell trying to get off the Island. He wasn't going through that shit again.

"You remember what happened on Rikers. It turned into a death trap." He tried reasoning to them.

"But, this place is run by the Government. They've got guns. Boats. Food." She turned around, telling the crowd, "I think we should go there."

The crowd started getting unruly and restless again. Many were already panicking and the situation only made it worse. Ed tried to quiet them down again, but they just spoke over him saying things like, you've got guns, you can protect yourself, and maybe they followed y'all here in the first place. That was enough for Kalene. She stood up.

"Everyone! Just shut the fuck up! Yeah, no doubt it's fucked up. But, trust me, panicking isn't where you want to be going right now. Trust me, I know. My family was murdered by those creatures in Chicago. We got hit the hardest. The ones who panicked were killed quickly. The ones who kept their heads survived." She turned towards Ed and said somberly, "And, we, at least I did relocate... here."

Ed sighed. Looking over the crowd, he said, "It has to be done in groups. It would be too risky to move everyone at one time."

An older man, also gray and his skin showing the signs of a man who had seen more yesterdays than he would tomorrows said, "He's right. There's no use in trying to take everyone. It would be risky to make a move like that," he looked around at some of the elderly, "especially for some of us."

Kalene stepped to him and said, "No, we wouldn't leave anyone behind."

He reached out and grabbed her by the hand gently and said, "Look. Realistically. We couldn't make a journey like that if everything was normal. Just leave us some food behind. Little ammo. We'll make it."

The same woman who'd been yelling earlier walked up to him. "I didn't mean anything-"

"No. You're good. What you're saying is correct."

"But, now the thing is. Who goes on the first wave?" the woman from earlier asked.

Everyone looked at Ed.

The elder that sat down from earlier rose back up and stepped towards the front. Ed stepped to the side. "Women. Children. Those elders that can make it." She looked around. "Are we in agreement?"

It came slowly, but it came. Everyone agreed unanimously. This was the plan. It was a go. They had to leave. Ed walked over to Kalene and sighed, saying, "Across Brooklyn and across the Brooklyn Bridge. Making our way into Midtown Manhattan. Then, find a way to travel to the Island." He looked around the room and did a mental count. "About what... three, four times?"

"We can do it."

"You know. Some won't make it."

"Maybe. But, most will."

"Yeah... most. But, I think everybody wants to be most."

A Plan...

Standing over the table was Ed, an elder by the name of Poochie and his partner, Curtis. Then, there was Kevin, Jamal, and Kalene. Poochie pointed to a route on the map on the table and said, "We take the Williamsburg Bridge and head up Second Avenue. It's quicker."

Ed scoped it out and said, "I thought that side of town was overrun?"

"It was. But, it's slowed down since, I've heard."

"He's right," Jamal chimed in. "Remember, we made a run over that way about a month ago."

"Yeah. We had to go to the Precinct over there."

"We got the guns and ammo. In and out. Didn't see anything."

"But, that was before they were able to come out in the day."

"But, who's to say that they're actually out everywhere? We don't know for sure," Curtis said.

"We don't." Ed looked around at everyone. "But, are we willing to take that type of chance?"

Kalene looked out the window at the buses that they were going to use for the journey and said to them, "We might not have a choice."

The buses that they were going to use belonged to the school across the street. They were parked in a lot across from it. They needed some repairs, but nothing major. When everything started happening, they were abandoned. Some tried to hide out inside the buses, but they were found and eventually slaughtered. No one had stepped foot in them since.

Right behind them was an abandoned building, and inside of there were creatures that had hunkered down. To command the bus, they would have to do several things. One. Clean out the bodies inside. Two. Repair the damage to them. Quietly. And three. Get everyone inside the bus quickly and quietly and haul ass before the creatures knew and could react. But, not one time, but several times.

"So. Another question." Poochie walked over towards the window looking out, then back at them and asked, "How do we decide who gets to go?"

"Good question," Kalene replied. She looked over at Ed, then Curtis. "Yeah. Who decides?"

JAMAL HAD FOUND THREE guys that were pretty good mechanics. He made a deal with them and relayed it back to Ed. They'd repair the bus, as long as their families got to go. They agreed to it.

Another issue they had was the fact that there wasn't just one bus but actually two. And, it was also brought up that maybe they could go for both. Curtis disagreed. Taking a chance and fixing one with what limited tools they had was a stretch, and the other issue was fuel. In particular, diesel fuel, so Ed and Kalene went out searching for that.

They didn't have to go too far. Curtis had told them that the hospital should have some. Probably stored for their generators in case of power failure. But, the whole thing was getting it. The hospital was a hotbed for the creatures. When they started coming to life, so to speak, the morgues were busier than a train depot. It was also where people that were infected had gone. Many died and there were literally hundreds of bodies there. So, when they came back to life, the hospitals were worse than the cemeteries. When they ventured out at night to feed, they ended up going back there.

Ed and Kalene knew it was going to be dangerous, so they agreed that they should be the only two. The less, the better.

It would possibly take about three trips to acquire enough fuel for a few runs, so they started out early.

Trapped...

The hospital they targeted was not far at all. Woodhull Hospital. One of the many progressive hospitals from the mid seventies. It had seen its fair share of nightmares from the area since. Heroin overdoses. Shootings from the surrounding projects and of course the scourge of cocaine that came through.

On Flushing Avenue and Broadway in Bushwick. A quick enough run. Starting early and real quiet, they made their way over there.

Once there, they kept the two five-gallon jugs they had secured to them, in hopes that the generators actually had fuel. They were not too hard to find. Ed figured everything should be towards the back. He remembered when the hospital was actually being built. He had done several part time gigs there with the local security back then, so he somewhat knew his way around.

He found them. Pretty huge but simple enough for him to navigate. He found a drainage tank below the excavation ledge was fitted with a pump for overflow. He opened the cap and took a sniff. Diesel fuel. He motioned to Kalene to pass the containers.

They quickly filled them up and hauled ass back to the Projects. They were able to make two trips with no hiccups. The third time isn't always a charm; they weren't so lucky.

They traced their same steps inside the hospital. The back entrance leading towards the maintenance area and boiler room. Real simple, they figured. But, two of the creatures had started to drift. They came from the other end of the basement. The morgue area. Ed and Kalene spotted them and they ducked off, but it wasn't the noise that attracted them their way. It was the smell of the diesel fuel.

Kalene had mistakenly spilled some, pouring it into a jug, and it had gotten on her. It was getting late and she didn't bother to change the shirt it spilled on.

The creature slowed down somewhere where they were hidden. Ed and Kalene remained deathly still. They were just about to leave their presence when one got a little bit more curious and peeped a little more; then, he spotted Ed. It screeched. The other one turned and started screeching as well. Ed yelled at Kalene. "Go ahead and fill up the other jug. I'll hold them off."

"Ok!" Kalene said and ran off towards the generator and started pumping fuel into the jug. One of them lunged at Ed and he sidestepped and stabbed it in the head. The other was coming at him as well. It was too late to pull the knife out of the other one's head, so he kicked at it and it fell backwards. Giving him enough time, he finally pulled the knife out.

He started to go for the kill, then stopped in his tracks when he heard more screeching and screams. He turned around and saw more coming their way. He hollered at Kalene to hurry. She was just about finished anyway and picked up the jugs and ran his way. They ran up to the fire escape, upstairs where they came in, and that's when the creatures started coming down in droves. They looked behind them and there were more coming into the basement.

Ed figured if they could make their way back out towards the back of the building. When the fuel trucks came in, they might have a chance.

There was a fenced area as well. They would have to scale it. But, they had no choice. Ed pointed towards the direction. It was their only chance. They ran towards it at a frantic pace. They kicked through the metal door that separated them. It busted open and they stopped dead in their tracks.

There were more of them. They looked their way and shrieked. As if calling the others. Making them aware of their location. Ed and Kalene back up slowly.

They were trapped.

Trapped...part 2

J amal looked up the street trying to see if he could spot Ed and Kalene on their way back. There was no one. He asked one of the mechanics, "Wonder why they're taking so long?"

The mechanic lifted his head up and looked around. "Don't know. It has been a while though."

"You think something may have happened to them?"

"Don't know. Maybe, we should check it out."

"Naw..." He looked at his watch and said. "Give it a little more time."

"Definitely, but before it gets too dark."

ED SPOTTED SOMETHING. An old steam boiler. The Maintenance at the hospital never got the chance to remove it, he figured because he spotted three brand new boilers that were piped into the existing system. This one wasn't. Maybe it could help them. On top of most older boilers was a man-sized hole used for maintenance inside of it. He stood up and looked to see if this was one of them. Yes, it has one, he said to himself.

He tapped Kalene on her shoulder and pointed towards it. "How do we get up there? And, what about these jugs?" she asked.

"Climbing on top is the easy part, just follow me. As far as the jugs. Leave them. We have no choice."

They ducked down lower some more, and started planning their move when they heard some creatures coming.

32

"We've got to make a move quickly. Staying in this spot... it's not good."

She nodded her head, okay. Then, secured the nozzle to the jugs and stuck them aside, out of the way. Ed pointed the way up top.

They made a break for it. Ed climbed on top of the cement foundation it was on. It was dug up, but it sat on three steel beams that weren't really secured. He jumped on top of it, and it kind of rocked a little. He steadied himself and, when it stopped, he climbed further towards the top. Kalene followed closely behind. Ed grabbed her by the hand and lifted her up to keep her close to him.

Once on top of the boiler, they had a good view of the basement and spotted another exit. But, they were also spotted as well. The creatures charged the boiler, and tried to climb on top of it. Ed and Kalene found the hole and it was uncovered, but Ed needed a way to seal it to keep the creatures from getting inside themselves.

He saw something once he looked inside. Steel plates. They climbed in and he used the steel plates, along with some bricks and pipe, to keep it secured. They moved closer towards the back end of the tight enclosure and waited.

The creatures jumped on top of the old boiler trying to get in, but there were too many, and they caused it to tip over. It started to roll off the steel beam foundation, and fell on its side. In the process, the hole was covered from the outside, and Ed and Kalene were stuck inside.

The steel pipes inside the structure kept the boiler intact, but the space, however, was confined. They could hear the creatures outside still trying to get in. Some had been squashed to death and the others started eating on them. Then, after a while, it got quiet. Ed tried pushing at the hole, but it was stuck. Something on the outside was pushing on it. "It's getting late. I know someone knows we're missing. Maybe, they'll come looking for us.", he said.

"That might be dangerous for them."

"True. We'll just wait it out at least until tomorrow. We'll figure something out."

"It's cold here."

"The metal. The steel. C'mon, get closer. We're going to have to keep ourselves warm tonight."

Kalene moved closer to Ed, and she could feel his warmth coming from his body. His heart was racing fast, because of the dangerous situation they were in. "Are you... scared?" she asked.

He looked deep into her eyes and said, "Yes. Since day one... day one."

She looked back at him and felt a connection. She kissed him then pulled back, awaiting a response. He hugged her and started kissing her back. She pulled him closer to her, feeling his heartbeat against her breasts, kissing him passionately. She hadn't felt this good in so long, and it had been awhile since she felt the touch of a man on her body, especially since the outbreak. Ed was a sense of security for her, and that was what pulled her to him in the first place. She needed that in this environment because she had no one else. She was alone.

Ed felt the same way she did but, in this environment, he knew it wouldn't be wise to take something like this to the next level. He had to think logically. He had to think about what was going on, right now. They looked in each other's eyes and stopped, knowing now was not the time. But, it still didn't stop Kalene from imagining and wanting, and Ed felt the same way.

Nowhere To Run...

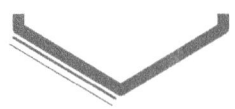

J amal strapped up. He loaded up his 12-gauge pump shotgun, and threw some extra loads in his jacket, then took a long deep breath. Kevin stepped up from behind him and asked, "Where are you going? It's getting dark out there."

"No doubt. But, Ed and Kalene aren't back yet."

Kevin looked out the window facing the direction of the hospital and said, "But, they might be on the way back now."

"It's been three hours...it's getting late."

Kevin walked over to his homeboy and patted him on the shoulder. "They might be doing a little something. You know. You can see the way that chick looks at him."

Jamal pushed his hand off his shoulder and said, "Naw... I don't think so."

Kevin knew that Jamal had developed feelings for Kalene, and he was hoping it was just one of those things but, as he now could see, it wasn't. "Alright. Hold up. Let me get my stuff."

"Naw. I got this."

"You got this? Get the fuck outta here. I know you in your feelings, but don't be a fool."

"Fool? You're calling me a fool!" He stepped at him with his fist balled up.

Kevin didn't move and looked him square in his eyes and said, "Look at you now. How you're reacting." He backed away and said, "We've been down together since kids. Been through all this crap and more. Even

35

coming down here from the Bronx when you wanted to check up on your peeps, and guy stuck. Stay here..." he sighed and continued saying, "but, if you go out there by yourself. Especially, if all you're thinking about is that broad, then cuz... yes, you're a fool."

Jamal unclenched his first and said solemnly, "I'll wait for you..."

On the way up to the hospital, the sun had eased down some. It wasn't a complete sunset but, in about another two hours, it was a wrap. They had enough time to look for them one way or another, and then make it back in time before the creatures came out full-fledged. With or without Ed and Kalene.

They eased into the hospital by way of the emergency room, and Jamal asked Kevin, "Where do you think they went?"

"Looking for fuel, more than likely. Probably the maintenance area. Or, wherever they fuel up the vehicles."

They looked around some and stopped when they approached the lobby, and that's when they spotted the directory. "It says the boiler room is in the basement. That's probably where they'll keep fuel of some sort." Jamal looked around and pointed. "Right there. Those stairs."

They made it over to the stairwell silently and cautiously looking around, eased down the steps, and then Kevin stopped and told Jamal to hold up. He peeped around a corner and saw some creatures lingering around. He put his finger to his mouth, letting him know to be silent. He eased back up and whispered, "Quite a few down there, just lingering."

"What else?"

"A lot of dust. Like, something happened."

"No sign of them, huh?"

"I haven't seen anything."

"We still have to look."

Kevin sighed. "Man, look. They could be on their way back." He checked his watch. "We're pushing for time as it is."

Jamal pushed past him. "I'm still looking." He eased around the corner and down the last flight of stairs. Gun pointed out in front and ducking down low. When he got to the last landing, he saw the boiler and how it had been toppled over. He realized that's where all the dust that lingered in the air had come from. Looking around some more, he spotted one of the jugs that Kalene had stashed.

He also saw some of the creatures, and they were pushing up against a hole or something. It looked like an entryway on top of the boiler. He crept further and noticed that there seemed to be a gathering. They weren't going to leave. They seemed to be waiting.

He wondered why, then he thought as he eased a little closer, he saw that the entryway was large enough for people to crawl in. Maybe, just maybe, they crawled inside. But, how could he know for sure?

He turned to let Kevin know, and he was right behind him observing the same thing. "Yeah. I see it too."

He pointed to the hole. Even if they went in after them. They'd have to move some of the concrete around so that if they were in there, they could make it out.

But, right now, they needed a diversion to draw the creatures away.

Jamal pointed towards a bay area where the large industrial structures were pulled in and out the facility. "I'll post up over there and try to draw them away. I'll start shouting. They'll come running my way and that should give you enough time to get them out, if they're in there."

"Naw. That's too dangerous."

"We don't have a choice. I can hold them off until you get them out; then, we can all handle them together."

Kevin sighed. "Damn! I don't like it, but we don't have time to argue." He looked out the overhead window and could see the sun was starting to set. "Let's go then."

Jamal stealthily crept around the side of the maintenance shop to the bay area. He posted up and tried climbing on top of a ledge to get a better spot. When he did, his leg kicked over a stool and it fell to the ground. All hell broke loose.

The creatures looked his way and screamed. It was like an alarm. They all started rushing his way. He scrambled up further on top of a pipe leading to a water main system above. Kevin held his ground, then eased over to the boiler which they'd now left unoccupied. Creeping around to the hole, he took the butt of his gun and tapped three times. He waited. Then, he tried three times again. Nothing. He was just about to leave and go help Jamal when he heard three taps come back.

Easing back, he then put his face to the enclosed hole and said, "It's me, Kevin. Ed? Kalene?"

Ed answered back, "Yeah. We're here."

"Ok. I'm going to have to move some of this concrete from around the entryway and then...we'll see if we can get you out."

"Yeah. There's something on the outside pushing against it."

"I got it."

Kevin pushed on the heavy steel beam that had flipped up and jammed the big concrete slab up in front of it. It wouldn't budge. He spotted a long, three-inch black steel pipe and figured he could use it as a wedge to hopefully pry back the concrete slab that was jammed against it. He wedged it in, then pushed at it a few times. It finally budged, then he hollered out to them, "Okay, I got it!"

Ed moved the steel he had blocking against the entryway from the inside, and he and Kalene climbed out.

Ed helped Kevin ease the steel wedge down so it wouldn't draw any attention to themselves. After that Kevin pointed over to where the creatures were trying to get at Jamal. Kalene gasped and immediately started over his way, but Ed stopped her. He pointed her towards the jugs. "Get the jugs." He looked at Kevin and said, "Look over there." He pointed towards the opening where they'd come in. "That way leads directly outside. Get the jugs, and I'll get Jamal."

Kalene pulled at Ed. "No, we'll go together." She reached for his hand caressingly. Ed reached out and kissed her hand. "I got this."

Ed started moving over towards Jamal and then Jamal spotted him. He opened fire on the creatures, drawing their attention from Ed. Ed shot at them from behind. They'd eliminated quite a few, allowing Jamal to ease down. He got up with Ed and shook his hand. "Is Kalene alright?"

"Yeah. She's making her way out with the fuel. Her and Kevin."

"Cool."

They started to run towards them, but one of the creatures attacked Jamal from behind. He wrestled with him, and Ed started kicking at him trying to get him off of him. Then, more of them came running towards them both and Ed fired what was left of his rounds. He dropped a few but more came.

The sun was now setting, and Jamal was now swarmed with them all over. Ed tried kicking and hitting them with everything he could grab, but he could see that Jamal had already been bitten. They were literally trying to eat him alive.

Kalene and Kevin heard the commotion and came running back. She screamed out, "Jamal!" That attracted the creature's attention their way.

Ed tried pulling her away, but she fought hard against him. "We gotta go, it's too late!"

Ed shouted at Kevin, "Let's go!"

Kevin turned and said, "No. That's my friend. Go ahead!"

Kalene called out to him, "No, please no!"

Ed grabbed her and shoved her towards the window, then picked up the jugs and said, "We gotta go. Now!"

They scrambled out the window they came in and ran. It was getting dark, and they could see the creatures coming out of their hiding spots. They continued running as hard and fast as they could until they made it back to the projects. Ed banged at the door. It was unshackled and opened. He and Kalene fell in, tired and breathing heavily. Curtis asked, "Where's Kevin? Jamal?"

Ed put his head down and Kalene cried. Suddenly, someone hollered out, "Look! Coming up the block. Running!"

Curtis looked out. "It's Kevin!"

Kevin had made it to the door and, as soon as they opened it, he dived through. There were a bunch of the creatures behind him.

He was bloody, so they all backed up and he said, "It's not mine." Then, he turned around to go upstairs, looked over at Kalene and said bitterly, "It's Jamal's."

The Gathering...

Crowded, and it was just as noisy as it was the first time they came together for a meeting. But, more restless this time, and the place was filled with anxiety. But finally, the tally was done. All the chips that were given out with the numbers on them had been collected.

Each person was given a number. A number that they only knew. Those chips with the numbers were put in a huge barrel. A barrel that was made to spin and subsequently mix up the chips.

Then came the elder; the same woman from before. It was her job to reach into the barrel and take out the chips; one at a time, until it reached 24. Then once more again, 24. Then, one more time, 24. Three times, just to make certain. That would be the number of people the bus would take to the Island. 72 people would be the start. Men, women, and children.

There were some that declined. Some were elderly. Some disabled. Some that were against leaving, thinking that it was safer in Brooklyn. The elderly woman looked over at Ed and said she was ready to give out the names, then, it got quiet.

The first group consisted of eight men: six women; seven children, and three elders. Not including the driver, rear security, a mechanic, and Ed and Kalene.

The first run would be in the morning. The only things to be carried were small bags of necessities, nothing heavy. Once the bus got back, there would be another group to go next. They agreed on that.

Ed caught up with Curtis and asked, "Do you think we'll make it?"

Curtis looked over at the bus and said matter of factly, "Sure. But, that's on a normal day, and this shit is anything but normal." He took a rag out of his back pocket and wiped some oil from his hands. "Shit, your guess is as good as mine, Ed," then walked off.

Ed stood there in deep thought, thinking about Roosevelt Island. He knew he had to get everyone on the bus there safely. They had to make their way up Broadway to the Williamsburg Bridge, cross into Manhattan, and then make their way up Second Avenue to the tram taking them to Roosevelt Island. The old Coast Guard station.

But, his main concern was not so much the route but the creatures along the route. Would they attack the bus? And, if they did, could they hold them off? That was his main concern.

He glanced over at Kevin. He knew he was still feeling fucked up about Jamal. They were tight. He wondered if he would still be down to ride shotgun on the second run. He figured now was a good time to ask.

"Yo, wassup Kevin. You alright?" Ed reached for his shoulder, and he shrugged it off.

"Yeah. I'm cool. Why?"

"Just figured I'd ask. I mean, I know you and Jamal were boys."

"Yeah. We...were pretty tight."

"I'm sorry about what happened."

Kevin turned and looked at him sideways. "I begged him to wait. To wait until the morning."

"That probably would have been best-"

Kevin gawked at him, then said, "You're kidding me, right." He turned facing him and pointed his finger in his chest. "He wanted to get that chic. Save her ass."

"Chic?"

"Yeah. The chic that you're fucking. That chic."

"Hold up. There's-"

"You see. For some God damned reason, he liked that fucking...chic, that you're fucking, so goddamn much that he risked his own damn life.

His life. And, now you say something fucking stupid like, he should have waited until the morning." Kevin looked at him sideways, then said, "Yeah. This way he wouldn't have interrupted y'all little fuck fest."

"Whoa, hold up Kevin." Ed got up in his face.

"What? What? I mean. Did I say something wrong?"

At that moment, Kalene came down the stairs overhearing some of what was said and asked, "Hey, what's wrong you two? Is everything alright?"

Kevin looked at Ed, then sucked his teeth. "Yeah. Thought so." He turned saying, "Everything is alright. Trust me. Everything is fucking alright," and walked off.

Kalene started to go after him, but Ed pulled her back. "Let him go. He's feeling bad about Jamal."

"Damn. Can you blame him?"

Ed watched as he walked off and said, "I can't blame him at all."

Another Episode...

The bus driver was in place, and Kalene was already posted in the back with a shotgun. Ed stood at the back entrance of the building, and Curtis came out from the lobby telling him, "Okay. They're ready."

Ed signaled to the bus driver to crank up and then told Curtis, "Tell them to come, now."

It was early. The sun hadn't quite made its way up yet, and the creatures were already making their way back into their hiding spots. There hadn't been much activity the night before aside from the few that would always look for openings. Banging on the door. Looking for scraps. Stuff like that.

The door opened at the back of the building, and everyone that was going ran out. At the same time, the bus cranked up, Ed and Curtis pulled up the rear. The building doors were then locked. There was no coming back. Ed secured the bus doors then told the driver, "Let's go."

Hearing the bus crank up drove the creatures back out into the streets. They screamed and ran towards it, but the driver stomped the gas. A few jumped in the way, but they were promptly run over. He didn't slow down until they were quite a ways away, and that's when Curtis had him slow down some to conserve fuel. So far, everything was okay.

Everyone on the bus had ducked down in their seats earlier, but now they were safe. The Sun had fully come up, and some were comfortable with peeping out the windows. The bus hauled ass across the bridge into Manhattan, and they felt a whole lot safer.

But, that wouldn't last long. Manhattan was swarmed with creatures too. Many walked around in the day trying to find places to escape the sunlight. That's when Ed told everyone to duck down some. The driver eased his way through a swarm of them here and there. A few even banged on the bus looking for a way in. Ed and Kalene crouched down some, waiting for any of them to try to hang on, but none did. They seemed to pretty much ignore them. They were too focused on trying to escape daylight

The driver wiped sweat from across his brow once the numbers started dwindling and kept going. Ed passed him some water and said, "You're doing good."

A few moments later, they were on Second Avenue. "Halfway there," Ed said.

They finally made it to the East River and the tram that they'd take across. However, as Ed and Chris looked closer, it looked to be partly damaged. Damaged to the point that they couldn't go across it. "It looks like it's been destroyed," Curtis said as he looked closer, analyzing the damage.

"Intentionally at that," Ed said.

The driver, Al Benida, stretched his neck looking, then he recalled. "Yeah, yeah. I remember. The creatures were trying to make their way over, and the people-"

"But, I thought no one lived over there."

"Naw. There were some. Small hippy type of group."

"Hipsters?"

"Yeah, yeah, whatever. They destroyed the tram to keep them from coming."

"So, how did they get on and off?" Curtis asked.

Al looked around towards the docks and spotted what he was looking for. "Over there." He pointed towards the docks where the ferry that was there was normally moored. The ramps were destroyed. But, off from the pier the ferry sat halfway across the inlet in the water. Ed spotted some activity onboard, and said. "Go over there."

They drove over and started waving at the people that were standing on deck trying to get their attention. Someone waved back, then shouted, "What can we do for you?"

"We'd like to get across, over to the Island."

After a pause and what seemed like a little discussion on their end, the same person hollered back, "No!"

Curtis was taken aback. What the hell? "Why not?"

"Well, for one, we don't even know who the hell you are. And two. Why should we?"

Ed looked at Curtis and said, "I thought you had this worked out."

Curtis looked back at him and said, "I thought I did too."

"Well, then, what the hell are we going to do? It's getting dark soon, and we need to make a move."

Curtis got off the bus and walked over towards the pier. Ed tried stopping him, but he pulled away from him. Ed convinced him to at least let him go with him, just in case. He at least agreed to that.

Kalene secured the doors once they got closer to the water. Once there, Curtis yelled out, "Let me speak to Jerry!"

"Who?"

Curtis shook his head and said, "Look. We're not going anyway until I speak with Jerry."

The ones that were on the boat huddled up, and then someone went inside the cabin. A few minutes later, he came back out with a short and stocky bearded man who smiled at Curtis and yelled, "About fucking time!"

"What kind of games are you guys playing?"

"They don't mean any harm but, hell, they don't know you. It's getting harder and harder to trust people."

"But, damn Jerry. I'm your fucking brother."

Ed twisted his neck around towards him. "Brother?"

"Yeah. My brother. Let's go back and pull the bus over and unload these people."

The ferry picked up its anchor and came closer towards the pier and docked. They tossed a line over, and Curtis and Ed pulled it closer. Kalene opened the bus door and the people came out and boarded the ferry. Curtis' brother stepped off and gave him a hug. "It's about time you came." He reached his hand out to Ed. "Jerry. I've been trying like hell to get my brother over here." He watched as the people boarded. "That's all you got?"

"No," Ed replied. "We've got more. We're bringing more back tomorrow."

"Ok-ok. Around the same time, right?"

"Just about."

He turned to board the ship and said, "Then, we'll be expecting you." He turned and boarded the ship, turned back around and asked, "How many times?"

Curtis put up two of his fingers and hollered back, "Two more!"

The ferry was untied from the pier and started drifting away, and Jerry hollered back at them. "Then, you better go now." He looked out into Manhattan. Place got really ugly close to dark. It's like zombie land or something." He waved and said, "Tomorrow."

Ed and them got back in the bus and Kalene said, "Well, so far, so good."

"Yeah, so far," Curtis said. "So far." He turned towards Al Benita and pointed. "Let's get back to Brooklyn before it gets too late."

The ride back was pretty uneventful. Ed did comment on the fact that there weren't as many creatures roaming about. He mentioned that that in itself was pretty strange, considering what had been going down the last few weeks. Curtis said that it seemed to be only happening down their way. But, Ed mentioned to him, what about Downtown Brooklyn?

The Move...

The next day the second pick climbed aboard the bus, and everything went fluid. Across the bridge into Manhattan; Second Avenue to the waterfront across from the Island; then, the ferry. They boarded the ferry and Jeremiah met them then took them across and, once again they left.

Curtis did, however, mention something strange. Not only did he not see any creatures; rats, dogs, no animal life, but also people. The living. He thought about mentioning it to his brother the next time he saw him.

Crossing back into Brooklyn, they ran into a roadblock. A few cars were turned on their sides into the street, causing Al to detour. Ed was curious, and had many questions about the cars, but there were no answers. He wanted to investigate, but Kalene advised against it. It was late in the day and she didn't think they should chance it. Curtis agreed.

They made it back with no real problems. Once inside the building and after securing the bus, Curtis walked over to Ed and asked, "What do you think was up with that roadblock?"

Ed looked at him and said, "Been thinking about that my damn self."

Al walked up on their conversation and asked. "You guys talking about that roadblock?"

"Yeah."

"Creepy as fuck, huh."

Curtis agreed then asked, "Is there another way? I mean, without going too far out the way and slowing us down."

Al thought about it for a minute then said, "There is. Get off Broadway and go down Hooper Street. Make the left, and then go about three-four blocks then make it back over to Broadway."

"But," Ed added. "By that time, we'll already be at the Bridge, so we might as well keep going straight and hit the rampway from there."

"Yeah, that would save some time."

"Ok." Curtis shook everyone's hand and turned to go upstairs. "It's a rap then. We'd better get some rest."

Al and Ed watched as Curtis bounced up the steps, then Al turned to him and said, "Don't like switching up like this late in the game, but I get it though."

"Tomorrow will be the last run anyway."

"What about the rest of the people staying here?"

Ed walked over to the window again, looking out across the street at the school. "We'll still leave them on the other bus, just in case they change their minds and want to leave."

"Good deal." Al yawned and said, "I'm tired, see you bright and early."

"No doubt." Ed watched him leave and then leaned up against the window looking out. Thinking to himself, maybe he should go upstairs and check things out. He also thought about going to sleep, but his only real thoughts were on Kalene. He couldn't get her off his mind, so he walked up the stairway quietly to the third floor, where she stayed. Hoping that maybe she was thinking the same.

Once he reached the door he started to knock, but hesitated. He eased back some thinking that maybe this whole thing was wrong. How could he commit to something like this? On this level?

Supposed something were to happen. To him. To her. Then what. With all this madness going on, it's not that it is so far -fetched. Besides, he thought, he already had too much going on. Too many responsibilities already.

He turned to leave and the door cracked open. He turned back around and eased forward peeping in. He could see Kalene walking towards the doorway to the bedroom. She was wearing a rope and nothing else. She turned around towards him, opened it up, and said. "When you close the door...behind you. Make sure It's locked."

The Move...2

Most of the riders going into Manhattan were already up. But, that wasn't what all the buzz was about this morning. Ed and Kevin were going at it. Kevin also had a notion to go see Kalene. He wanted to talk to her about the feelings Jamal had for her. He knocked on the door and Ed answered. In his shorts. And, that's what triggered him.

Ed asked why they went to the hospital that evening anyway. He knew he was wrong telling him he should have waited; saying that's what he would have done, but it was done. Kevin mentioned that if he knew he was fucking Kalene, he still would have went. Ed said that he wouldn't have, so Kevin punched him in the mouth, and Ed deserved that.

They wrestled around some on the ground until Kalene stormed out and came in between them, stopping them, but not the mean mugging. Kevin told her about Jamal, and she stormed back into her apartment and slammed the door behind her. Ed knocked hard, asking her if she was okay. She opened it some and handed him his clothes and said, "Please, go. This was a mistake."

"Mistake? No!"

"Ed! Please go. I'll see you in a few. I'll be ready for the bus ride."

"So, that's it?" Ed said as he stood there with his clothes in his hand.

"This was a mistake, Ed. A big mistake." She looked over his shoulder at Kevin who was standing there and said, "Both of you...just leave." Then, she shut the door.

Ed stood there for a minute, then turned and looked at Kevin smugly and said to him, "You got what you wanted!" and brushed past him.

Kevin said, "Naw. You got it fucked up. What I want is my homeboy back." He looked at Ed going into the staircase and shouted, "Should have been you... and not him!"

Kalene opened the door slightly. She wanted to say something to Kevin but, instead, he just turned, looked at her, and said under his breath, "Fuck... ain't no need to talk about it now. Enough has been said already and my boy is still dead." He walked off.

EVERYTHING WAS SET in motion. Everyone involved in the move was up and ready to go. The bus had been fueled with the last bit that was left. The only thing needed to do now was load.

After the bus was loaded and everything mapped out, Ed, Curtis and the bus driver, Al, were ready to go. As soon as they got packed up, Kevin ran up to the bus.

"I want to go on this trip. I'm ready to go."

Ed looked at him strangely and asked, "Why? I thought you were staying here. Why do you want to leave now?"

"I mean, why not?" He looked at them and said, "Why should I stay? Jamal is dead. I mean, this ain't my hood, so I might as well move on. That's enough for me."

Kalene said, "I thought you wanted to help these people."

"People? You stay and help them. Since you are so much into..." he glanced over at Ed, "helping motherfuckers."

Ed started to speak out, but Curtis cut him off and said, "Well, come on then. We can always use another hand." He yelled out, "Let's pack this bus! Let's go! Let's get this day started!"

Once they got the bus started and squared away, everyone said their goodbyes. They started moving out. By the time they got on Broadway, the ride was going smooth and it seemed like it was going to stay that way.

No Going Back...

It was just around Hewes Street in Williamsburg right before they got to the bridge that something strange happened. They saw that the creatures were starting to move about in the open, which was the norm, but just not in broad daylight.

Al stopped the bus and pointed at them. "You see what the hell is going on. The fuck. It looks like they're coming out of the woodworks."

Ed said, "Yeah. Like they are trying to form some sort of blockade or something."

"What the hell do you think is going on?"

"I don't know what the hell's going on, but I know one thing. We need to stay low."

Ed told everybody to get down. "Play the floor everybody and, Al, just go ahead...real slow and see what's going to happen but, know that if we need to run through them, that's what we're going to do." He turned and started telling Kalene and Kevin, "If we need to stop. Open fire on everything that moves. We'll need to open up the roadway, so just let go of everything you got until you run out of ammunition. Hell, this is the last run anyway."

"You got it," Kevin responded. He posted up towards the right hand side of the bus facing the street. He poked his AK-47 out through the steel bars they had welded together and was cocked and loaded. He gave Ed the thumbs up.

Kalene played the backside, in case they tried climbing on top from behind. Ed and Curtis stayed posted up front, loaded themselves. Ed looked over at Al and said, "Let's go."

Al moved the bus slowly up the street at first. A few of the creatures stopped and peeped, then went back to their own business, wandering indiscriminately. They drove a few blocks and only had a half mile or so to go to the bridge. Then, out of nowhere, one of the creatures ran straight at the bus. Then another. Then, two more. Al had to run them over, and that slowed the bus down some.

Ed yelled at him, "Step on it!"

Al yelled back at him, "I'm trying."

Kevin pointed to a building. "Oh shit. Check this out y'all!"

They looked and it seemed like dozens were pouring out the building, running towards them.

Ed scrambled over his way and pointed his gun out the window and said, "Shoot!"

They started shooting and dropped quite a few of them, and Al eventually got the bus moving again. Curtis yelled out, "Damn it, they're starting to come from the other side now!"

Ed turned and yelled. "It's a set up!"

"Damn right it is!"

The creatures started to run at the front of the bus, and Al stomped on the gas. He managed again to run over a few, but one of them dived at the window. It cracked some. Another one jumped and did the same thing. Curtis started shooting. Now, the windshield was compromised. It didn't take long for one more to jump through it. And when one did, it dove straight for Al.

Al yelled as he fought it off as best he could. Curtis tried pushing it back out, and then one of the creatures managed to take a bite out of Al's arm. He started bleeding. "Damn!" Curtis yelled out.

The bus had stopped and more started rushing towards them. Al shook his head in despair as he looked at his arm and said, "It's over for me." He got up and dove through the window and started fighting them off. They started to chase him. Next thing you know, he was covered with a bunch of them but, still, he managed to stay on his feet long enough to divert them away from the bus.

Curtis jumped behind the wheel and stomped the gas. They finally got away. A few blocks up Broadway, it was the same thing. "This is organized. Someone has to be setting us up," he said.

"I think someone has been setting us up all along!" Kevin yelled. "Those things knew we were coming."

"But, why didn't they attack us until now? Why now?"

"Don't know, but we're almost out of ammo." Kevin turned to Ed. "What do we do now?"

Ed looked down at the people on the floor scared and shaking. He didn't have an answer. But, one thing he definitely knew was that they couldn't stay there forever. He turned and looked at Kalene, then Kevin and nodded. "Fight...fight."

Kevin nodded. He had to put aside his differences. He answered, "Well. That's what Jamal would do."

Kalene loaded the last of her ammo and said, "It is what it is."

Curtis looked around at them, then told the passengers, "Keep your head down. Don't look up." He revved up the engine and said, "And, hold on to something because it's going to get a little ruff from here on out."

The bus swerved as it took off. Curtis stomped the gas and drove hard, running over and dodging past creatures as they made it to the beginning of the bridge. A couple of cars were partially blocking the entrance. Curtis yelled out and slammed into them, making a way through. Ed and Kevin fired round after round cutting down creatures as they ran after them, and some even hurled their bodies at the bus in an attempt to try and stop them. Kalene kept shooting as they tried hanging on.

Finally, they made it on the bridge. Kalene hollered at them. "Oh shit. Check this out." She pointed towards a swarm of creatures coming from out buildings and making their way up Broadway, where they'd just left.

"Oh, my God, they're about to raid the projects."

"We should go back and warn them."

Curtis kept driving. He said solemnly, "No." He pointed to the gas tank. "We got enough to either go back or go forward. But, not both."

Everyone looked at Ed. They couldn't say anything. He was right.

Curtis stopped the bus and asked, "What is it? What are we going to do?"

Ed looked at the people on the floor. Scared. Shaking. He looked back watching the swarm head towards the projects, then at Kevin and said, "It never gets easier."

Kevin nodded his head. "Yeah, I see."

Ed said, "We go...forward."

It is what it is.

The ride was slow. No one spoke. There was nothing really to say. Ed kept his head focused on going across. Kalene tried her best to comfort the people onboard. Once they made it on the other side, Kevin stepped to Curtis and said, "Stop the bus."

Curtis asked, "Stop the bus? For what?"

Kevin looked over at Ed and said, "I'm getting off."

"Getting off? What, are you kidding me?"

"Naw bruh. This is as far as I go." He looked into Manhattan. "I got it from here."

Ed moved closer to him and guided him towards a corner. "Look. I apologize. But, you don't have to take it this far."

Kevin said, "It's not about you. Things happen bruh. It's about me. Moving on."

Kalene walked towards him. "Kevin, you don't have to do this."

Kevin smiled and hugged her. "Actually, I do. Look, everything is good." He glanced over at Ed. "The big guy. He got y'all. He knows what he's doing."

"But," Ed said, "I don't have any ammo to give you. No weapons." Kevin pointed towards Police Plaza. "Yeah. But, I'm sure that place does. Besides." He pulled out his machete. "Jamal left me this. Hell, it worked for him. Shit, it'll work for me too."

Curtis opened the door and Kevin jumped out with his bag, waved them off, and started walking off. Ed looked down bitterly and said, "Let's go."

Curtis cranked up the bus and took off towards Second Avenue and hoped like all hell that they wouldn't run into another swarm of creatures.

Kalene watched somberly as Kevin disappeared from out of view. Ed walked up behind her and said, "That's what he wanted to do."

"That's true. But, I can't help thinking that maybe it was my actions that caused it."

Ed sighed and said, "Kalene, one thing's for certain. We're not God."

"Yeah. What kind of God would create this type of madness?"

"A mad...God."

Kevin's Last Song...

Kevin walked a few blocks towards the park leading towards Police Plaza. His mind heavy in guilt. He wasn't quite sure if he should have gotten off the bus, but he made a stance; he tried reasoning to himself. He was still feeling some sort of way about the loss of Jamal, and he was feeling some sort of way about Ed. It wasn't quite right the way he handled the whole situation. Maybe he was just jealous of Kalene too. Jamal paid her more attention than him. He saw that he was losing his friend. Now, he was gone forever.

He spotted a bench along the grass and sat looking around at the quiet. In silence. He wondered where he would go now. Probably back uptown. Suddenly, he heard a sound, then turned. He saw nothing. Then, another sound. He turned the other way, and they were already right up on him. One grabbed at him, and Kevin slid underneath him. He tried reaching for his machete, but another one grabbed a hold of his arm and bit down. Kevin dropped it. Another creature jumped on him, causing them both to fall to the ground. Others hearing the sounds came running where they were. Screaming, shrieking in a mad frenzy.

Kevin managed to fight them long enough to get to his feet and run. He ran towards the bridge. His arm was bleeding heavily, but he fought through the pain. He figured he'd try to run underneath the bridge. Hide out. He ran down a gulley, but it was sealed off by a chain linked fence and they were hot on his tail. He climbed up the embankment and made his way to the top of the walkway on the bridge. Running, but he kept falling. He was losing a lot of blood.

One of them had managed to catch him from behind, and Kevin fought for his life. Then, before he knew it, he was surrounded. They started to swarm towards him and Kevin put up his good hand standing in a defensive stance, ready for anything. He'd wished he'd at least gotten close to the water. He'd dive off. He'd rather kill himself instead of getting eaten by these monsters, or even worse. Turning into one of them.

He never saw it coming. And, it was best for him that he had not. His head was pierced through by a 40 caliber round. He staggered some, then dropped dead to the ground. He wouldn't be able to come back now. But, it still didn't stop the creatures from devouring his flesh.

Ed stood atop the bus. He lowered his rifle and his head. It needed to be done. He climbed down into the bus and told Curtis that it was done. He looked towards the back at Kalene and nodded solemnly. Curtis cranked the bus back up and kept going.

Kalene had begged them to go back and pick up Kevin. She didn't want him to be on his own. Ed agreed. He also figured he could use a good man like Kevin anyway. They could always patch up their differences another time. But, by the time they'd reached him, it was too late.

A mercy bullet to the head. It was a decision that they all agreed on. A decision they'd want one of them to make if it was one of them. But, Kalene couldn't swallow it, thinking it was all her fault. Another bad decision, she kept thinking over and over as she sobbed bitterly. But, for Kevin. It was the best decision.

A New Day...?

The very sobering ride didn't take long. Before they knew it, they were at the dock waiting for the Ferry to arrive. The passengers exited the bus and hugged the others that they knew. And, for once in a very long while, it was a joyous day.

Ed walked off to the side of the pier in thought. Kalene spotted him and started to go over to him, but Curtis stopped her. "Give him some space right now. He needs it." Kalene nodded. She needed some space as well. Her headaches were getting worse. She'd taken the antiviral drug that they had given her in Chicago. It was supposed to work against the bacterial infection. The coming back to life from the dead kind. She never found out the end results of it because the base had been overrun.

Other than the headaches, she didn't have any other symptoms. But, now, they were more intense. She wanted to confide in Ed, at least give him a heads up. But, she held back, thinking that it could also be a result of stress.

Ed watched as the Ferry docked, then waved at the Ferry Captain. Turning towards the City, he watched the skyline as it turned a dull image. He noticed a lot of that lately. He figured it was a lack of clean air, or maybe from the bodies that had not turned and laid rotting in the streets. The fumes were horrendous.

Fires still burned from cesspools of gas and methane that still lingered about the air. More times than often, he and the others were forced to wear gas masks when they went out. Sniffing at the air, it seemed like it was about to be one of those times.

He had some masks stocked, but he still wondered if he had enough for everyone. Hopefully they had enough on the Island. He made a mental note to inquire about it once he got there.

Something caught his eye. One of the buildings. A window. He noticed someone was standing in the window. Could it be a survivor? He squinted, trying to get a better visual. A man. White man. He squinted some more, and the figure moved, and he got a good look at his face. The features on his face were scarred. Ragged. His eyes were dark red. Ed's mouth dropped. It was a creature. And it was watching them. Intently.

Ed turned to call Curtis and, when he came over, he pointed towards the building up at the window. It, or whoever it was, was gone. "I swear Curtis. It was just watching us."

"I thought those damn things didn't think. I mean, after all, aren't they dead?"

Ed rubbed his chin. "Supposedly..."

Curtis rubbed his shoulder and said, "You need some rest Ed. Been through a lot of shit lately."

Ed turned his way, acknowledging what he said with a smile answering. "You might be right."

Curtis walked off towards the Ferry. Ed did tell him he'd be there in a minute, and he acknowledged that he did need the rest. He figured once he got over on the Island he'd chill for a bit. It was time anyway. He did all he could do. And, Jamal's death kind of worked on him.

He didn't sign up for this leadership thing. He kind of fell into it. Maybe it was time for him to fall out of it. Chill.

Kalene helped move whatever she could from off the bus. At times, succumbing to bouts of coughing. Curtis asked how she was doing and she responded by saying that she was well. He told her when she got to the Island, she should be looked at. Kalene agreed but, deep down inside, she really didn't want to. She kept thinking about her brother and his symptoms.

After boarding, the Ferry left the dock soon after. Ed stood along the side with Curtis and asked him about his brother. Curtis was curious himself. "I'm not sure. I asked about him, and no one seemed to be able to give me a solid answer. I hope he's alright."

"Probably so. Maybe he just couldn't make the trip over today."

"Maybe."

They got closer to the Island and he asked, "So. What's the deal with this place?"

"It's a safe haven of sorts. Keeps those monsters away." He pointed towards the perimeter of the Island. "As you can see. They have people watching at all times. Making sure no one comes in. As well as on and off the Island." He pointed towards the razor wire along the shore. "It's all around the Island, except when the boat comes through. And as you can see. That's armed."

Ed watched as the ferry was waved through an opening surrounded by barbed wire. He was relieved to see the armed men. Maybe, now, he could relax and let someone else put in the work.

He looked back towards the mainland. It was getting dark. He watched as the creatures came out of their respective shelters. Some headed towards the bus that stayed parked at the pier. They'll more than likely tear it up, he thought, but then something strange happened. It was cranked up. He found Curtis and pointed towards it.

"Yeah. That's definitely strange."

"Did we leave anyone behind?"

"No. Not according to the count. Might just be a survivor."

"Might be. But, whoever it is, why didn't they just reveal themselves to us?" Ed asked as he looked up at the building from earlier. "I wonder why."

They both watched as the bus turned off, and one of the occupants of the bus came over and said, "What the hell was that? Somebody trying to drive the bus away?"

Not wanting to cause any alarm, Ed glanced over at Curtis and said, "Uh... yeah. Believe it was a survivor."

"A survivor? I thought we were the only ones."

Curtis turned towards him and said, "Uh...no. Just some people. They'll be back." He guided him towards the front of the boat, pointing towards the Island. "Don't worry about that. Look. Your new home!"

He turned around once more, then shrugged his shoulders and turned back towards the Island as the Ferry started to dock. "Yeah. New home."

Curtis turned towards Ed and said, "C'mon. Don't worry about it. We'll check into it later. Maybe these guys on this side know something."

Ed nodded as they started walking to the gangway. "Maybe. It's not my headache anymore anyway."

THE FIGURE ON THE BUS stepped off and walked into an abandoned garage underneath a building. The same building Ed saw the figure in the window from earlier. The driver walked up the stairs into the lobby inside the building and gave the same man from earlier that Ed had seen in the window, the keys.

Too Many Questions...

Ed, Kalene, and Curtis were shown to their quarters. The place where they were staying was a three-story apartment complex, with two and three bedroom apartments. It had a nice sized lobby with a lounge and several small private dayrooms. There were several large screen TV's on the wall. Not that that would do any good, being there wasn't any television programming, but he did notice a DVD player. There may have been movies to pass the time.

Children were scattered about, and they played. They were not permitted to go outside however without permission or even an escort, for that matter. The adults hung out mostly among themselves. Reading. Looking outside, and conversing in what seemed to be pleasant conversation. It seemed like a decent place. And, it was pretty clean.

But, there was one question he had that nagged at him. Where was Jeremiah? He asked Curtis and even he didn't know. Then, he was told that he was busy on the other side of the Island. And, he was also told that he'd be in touch with him soon. Right then, they both knew that was strange.

"We'll give it a day or so."

"Then, we'll go look for ourselves."

Curtis started looking around at people and said, "You know something just doesn't feel right."

"I know. Too damn perfect."

"For real."

KALENE WALKED ALONG the shore checking out the perimeter. About ten feet into the water, it was gated with barbed wire strung around the top. Along the base of it were rocks with razors embedded on them. She guessed that was to make sure no one was able to climb in over the top.

She watched as the children played. She did however notice that there weren't any pets around. But, she hasn't seen much of that since this epidemic began anyway. She also noticed that there weren't any newborn babies either. Thinking further, she realized that she hadn't seen a newborn baby in months.

She wondered if she should stay. Maybe, have some sort of life. Be free of the running. The killing. The creatures. It sure seemed like a good plan. She spotted a bench and sat, staring off into the water. Suddenly, she felt a massive pain inside her head, along the temples. She screamed out some, then rubbed at them. Her eyes fluttered rapidly and she started having a seizure.

Someone spotted her and rushed her back to the dorm. A few hours later, she awoke inside a room. It was small. Like a jail cell. She got up and ran to the door, looking out the small window. Across from her, and up and down. She yelled out, but nobody responded.

Then, she looked at the door across from her and watched as someone slowly appeared to the window. It looked like one of the creatures. But, it didn't seem like it was fully developed yet. Almost looking to be half-human of sorts. She backed away from the window against the bed and fell to the floor crying out. Now what!

A FEW DAYS HAD PASSED, and Ed hadn't seen or heard from Kalene. He searched around the facility and couldn't find her. He asked around and no one knew who she was. He knew something was wrong. He caught up with Curtis and he said the same thing. A few people that they brought over were also missing. And, he still hadn't heard from his brother, Jeremiah.

"Where's the guns?" he asked Curtis.

"Hell if I know. They took them from us when we got off the Ferry."

"There must be an ammunition storage around here somewhere. There's no way they don't have any weapons."

"I agree."

They noticed that they were being watched closely. Most of the people now stayed their distance away from them as well.

"Something ain't right."

"Yo. Go pack a bag and meet me back in front of the building."

"Why?" Ed asked.

"Because we're getting the fuck out of here!"

"Damn right!"

They both disappeared up to their rooms.

It's Going Down...

Someone tapped on Kalene's door. She got up and turned toward it. It was an armed guard with a nurse. The guard ordered her to back away from the door; then, he opened up the door, pointing his rifle her way. "Turn around and put your hands up!"

She did, and he quickly searched her up and down. The nurse grabbed her arm and checked for a vein. Kalene started to pull away and asked her, "What are you doing? Why am I here?"

The guard poked her in the ribs with the butt of his gun and said, "Shut up!"

"Where the hell am I?"

"Didn't I say shut the hell up!" He went to poke her again and Kalene decided she'd had enough. She sidestepped, catching him off balance. She snatched the rifle from out his grip and spun it around, pointing it at him and the nurse. "Now, both of you! Get towards the back!"

They complied. The guard said, "Look. You won't get too far!"

"Am I still on the Island!"

"Yes!" the nurse said. "But, they won't let you off."

"The hell they won't!"

"You're sick!"

"I'm what." Kalene stopped.

"You're infected."

"No, I'm not."

The nurse started approaching her slowly, telling her. "The headaches. The seizures. It's starting to take."

"What's starting to take? What are you talking about?"

She started to point the gun at her and the nurse yelled, "7.3000!"

"What?"

"The 7.3000 virus. Evidently, at some point, you were injected with it."

Kalene remembered. When she was at the base with her mother and her brother.

"It was an antiviral drug. But, it doesn't work. It will make you turn...eventually."

"Turn?" Kalene started backing towards the door. "I'm good, trust me."

"For now. But, eventually, you'll turn. And, what will make it worse is. You'll still think. Might even look the same, but you'll be a creature. Please, let us help you."

Kalene looked up and down at the doors at some of the faces that started to approach the windows. "Doesn't look like you're helping anyone!"

The guard jumped towards her, and Kalene shot him. The nurse started to move towards her as well, and Kalene backed out the door and shut it. Then, she locked it. The nurse banged furiously. "You'll be a monster! You'll never leave this Island alive!"

Kalene turned and ran towards the exit. She had to find Ed.

By the time Ed and Curtis made it back downstairs, a crowd of people had gathered. They were pointing security their way. "Looks like trouble," Ed said.

Curtis nudged him towards the exit. "Let's get out of here."

It was blocked off by security, and they started heading towards them. Ed and Curtis were backed into a corner.

They put up their hands and took a stance, ready to fight. Then, gunfire erupted behind them. "Alright, drop to the ground!"

It was Kalene.

The security that had surrounded Ed and Curtis turned towards her and they both dived to the floor. They knew what was coming next. Kalene started shooting at them. Some were able to scatter and get away but, the ones who didn't, Ed and Curtis grabbed for their guns.

Ed gave the high sign to Kalene to cover the entrance, and she did. They ran towards it. Curtis fell. He'd been shot. Ed reached down and helped him up as they ran out the building. Curtis yelled out. "Now what!"

Kalene pointed towards the pier and said, "That's the only way."

"The Ferry? It's probably more guarded than the Island."

"We'll have to take that chance."

Curtis caught a round to the shoulder, but the bullet went straight through. He was still able to brandish a gun. Kalene and Ed were able to get to a toolshed posted across from the Ferry. The guards were starting to gather and roll on them.

"What are we going to do Ed?" Kalene asked.

"Well. We can't swim off this damn Island. And, we're going to catch hell trying to take the Ferry."

Curtis loaded his gun and said, "Then, I guess we have to make the best of it."

The guards started coming their way. The ones that were in the Ferry pointed their guns their way as well. Kalene pointed towards the building she'd just left and yelled, "Look!"

Creatures started coming out the front in droves.

"Where'd they come from?"

"That's where they had me held. There's a bunch of people locked in cells inside of there."

"What was going on in there?"

"They were experimenting. Trying to inject people with drugs."

"Drugs?"

She rubbed the side of her arm and said, "The vaccine. From when it first happened. The 7.3000."

"The cure."

"That's what they said it was. But, it might not have been."

Curtis interjected, "It was just another goddamn virus! That's all it was!" He watched as the guards started running out in their direction. "And, all this time, all they did was experiment with people they brought over!"

"Damn!"

"Damn right!"

The guards turned from them and started shooting at the creatures. They had started attacking the residents in the building. Some of the guards from the Ferry started running that way as well. They'd completely forgotten about Ed and them. They saw their shot and scrambled on board the boat. "Who knows how to drive this damn thing!"

Out of the shadows stepped Jeremiah, "I do."

Kalene's Sad Song...

Curtis rushed him. "Damn good to see you. What happened to you?"

"They tried to make me take the shot they were giving everyone. When I refused, they held me prisoner here. They didn't want me to say anything to anyone."

"Why didn't they take you to the building where they took me?"

"They were. Today. But all this craziness started happening."

The Island had exploded into a war zone. The creatures were attacking everyone. Men. Women. And even children.

"Well, we better go then, before they come this way," Curtis said.

"Too late." Kalene pointed towards the swarm of creatures that started approaching them.

"Pull up the anchor and untie us from the pier. I'll do the rest. And, oh yeah. They're more guns downstairs. We're damn sure going to need them."

They watched somberly from the Ferry as the onslaught continued. They managed to get the boat away from the pier out into the open waters before the creatures got to them.

Ed and Curtis stayed topside along with their weapons, keeping watch. A few had attempted to rush into the waters after them, but they picked them off.

Now, it was a matter of where to go.

"I guess we'll go back into the City," Curtis suggested.

"Yeah. We can. Or, we can just leave. Go somewhere else," Jeremiah said to him.

"Where can we go with a damn Ferry?"

"You'd be surprised."

"How about fuel?"

"There are a few fuel stops along the inlet. We'll go north up into Canada, perhaps."

"It'll be cold as shit, and we don't have the supplies."

"Ok. Then South."

Curtis thought for a second and said, "Yeah, that sounds cool."

"But, we still have to go to the City," Ed said to them.

"For what?"

"Supplies. Food."

"You're right. We'll go. In and out."

"Sounds like a plan."

They heard something downstairs and Ed looked around and asked, "Where's Kalene?"

They rushed downstairs, and Kalene was stumbling around, holding her head and screaming out in pain. "Oh, my God. It hurts so bad!"

Ed rushed over to her, trying to hold her down. "What's wrong?"

Kalene's eyes had turned bloodshot red. She started grabbing at her skin. Then, at her hair, pulling it out. Ed jumped back. Her gums started bleeding, and then she lunged at him. Fighting her off, Curtis came over to help him, and he said, "She's turning into one of those creatures."

She rubbed at her arm, and then Curtis pulled up her sleeves. "They injected her with something."

"Damn," Ed said. "We have to get her some help. Get some rope and we'll tie her down."

They did. Once they got upstairs, Jeremiah said to Ed, "Bruh, there is no help. She's turning into one of those things."

"No, we can help her. There's got to be a way."

Curtis patted him on the back. "There is no cure."

Ed looked up at them. Tears had welled up in his eyes. "So, what do we do?"

Jeremiah handed Curtis a gun and said, "I think you know."

Curtis held his head down and said, "I'll do it."

Ed stopped him and said, "No. I got it. She was my friend."

Curtis and Jeremiah backed away and started going upstairs topside, and Jeremiah said to him, "We still need to go into the City... for supplies."

Ed stopped and just nodded his head. "Okay."

He stepped into the small cabin where Kalene was being held. She was breathing heavily, and her head was hung down. Ed could tell that she had fought hard against the straps that held her restrained. Her wrists were swollen. He closed the door back behind him. "Kalene? Kalene?"

She lifted her head up slowly. Ed backed away some. "Yes. I'm still here."

"You're infected. They want me to come down and uh..."

"Kill me."

"You seem to be okay now. Maybe you were just sick."

"Maybe. But, maybe..."

Ed got closer up on her, trying to hear. She lunged at him and he fell back against the wall. "What the hell!" Her teeth gnashed out at him. Her eyes were bloody red, and she snarled. "You're the sick ones!"

Ed got up to his feet. He glanced at the gun he'd just dropped, and she also looked at it and started to plead. "Ed. I'm okay. I just need some rest. I'm not one of those creatures."

"How can I tell? How can I be sure?"

She gagged, like she was throwing up. Ed looked around for a bucket. Finding one, he slid it her way. She tried leaning forward but couldn't. "Ed, please help me..."

Ed leaned forward some, pushing it closer towards her. She lunged again. This time, the chair she was in fell forward towards him. Ed tried getting out of the way, but it was too late. She fell on top of him and started biting at him. Ed finally fought her off and kicked her away, and lunged for his gun.

Kalene fought with the rope around her arms that were now loosened, and she got free. She got up and yelled at Ed, "Don't fight it Ed. It's beautiful. You can be free-"

Her head took two slugs. Ed gasped in horror because he hadn't yet reached for his gun. He looked up and saw it was Curtis. "Didn't know if you could do it. Figured I'd check on you. I'm glad I did."

He reached for his arm to help him up. "Nothing... personal."

He looked at the downed body that once was Kalene. A woman he thoroughly had love for and said, "Nothing personal."

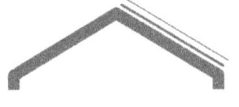

Somewhere Better...

E d knew it would take a while, so he had to move fast. He found a garage and started rummaging in and out of vehicles, looking for one that was drivable. He finally found one, but he had to drag the stink decaying carcass that was probably once the owner out.

The stench inside was horrible but, once he got moving and opened all the windows, it became bearable.

His destination. Brooklyn. Bushwick Projects. He'd remembered that they still had access to the gas from the hospital. He figured if he could rig up the bus that they'd left behind, he might make it into a gas bomb of sorts. Maybe that would be enough to sink the ferry and hopefully kill their plans.

But it still weighed on his mind. Were the ones running things human? How did that happen?

About a block away from the projects, he saw that the area was in ruins. Bodies were all over the street. Dead. Half-eaten body parts. It was a massacre. He got further up to the building and noticed some activity around the doorway. Maybe somebody or someone was still around. He cruised slowly towards the building and then slowed down.

He saw them. A group of creatures. They were still eating on bodies. Somehow, they'd broken through the defenses that had been set up.

Ed stopped the bus. He crouched down on the floor. He was already across the street from the other bus and got the chance to look at it as he drove past. It seemed to be intact. He wondered, why didn't they use it to escape?

He'd have to figure that out later. His biggest problem was to find the couple of gallons of gas that they had accumulated. Where did they put them? He pondered. He opened the door slightly and then pulled back slowly. He'd heard something. It was one creature, and he spotted the bus. He looked around for some movement and, not seeing any, he continued to rummage through the dead flesh. Eating off the carcasses like a vulture.

Ed continued to open the door slowly and, keeping his head down, he ran over to the other bus. He snatched the door open. Nothing. That was good. He made his way inside quietly and started searching for the key. It wasn't in the ignition. He reached under the seat and still found nothing.

Then he heard a sound. He ducked down and reached for his gun and aimed towards the door. There was someone; he looked harder. It was a teenage boy, and he was also crouched down. He was dirty and looked like he hadn't eaten in a while. He spotted Ed and then reached into his pocket and pulled out some keys.

"Looking for these?"

The bus keys. Ed eased towards him and asked, "Yeah. Who are you?"

"Alfonso. But people call me Fonzo."

"Did you live around here?"

He pointed to the other building next to the one where Ed had stayed. "There. 869."

"Yeah, yeah. What happened here?"

"I remember you. I remembered the meeting about leaving." He looked off and continued, "There was a big argument between the people who lived in the buildings. Some wanted to leave. To go where you went. So, they made a plan. But, the people who lived in your building felt that they should leave first. The other people felt that if they did, then they would not come back for the rest of them," he turned towards Ed, "like y'all did."

"But they wanted to stay."

"Only a few..."

"So..." He pointed towards the buildings. "What happened?"

"Fighting. Double crossing each other. Then, one night, someone came from your building bust, opened the door from our building and all hell broke loose."

Ed just shook his head in disgust. He had a good idea what had happened next. "They let the creatures in."

"Yes."

"But what about the rest...of the buildings? The tenants?"

"They all started fighting, too." He handed Ed the keys. "All for this one bus."

"Fools."

"Yeah, but what happened to you? Your people?"

Ed only stared blankly at the boy. The boy looked off. He could see a tear run down his eye, and he already knew the answer. Ed asked him. "Do you have any family?"

He shook his head no.

"Well. You might as well come with me. I'm going to need help to siphon all the gas we can find. Put it inside the other bus. Then, hopefully, find the other containers."

"Then...do we leave?"

He looked at the boy, and he finally smiled. "That's the plan." He'd finally seen a little hope in him. He turned back around and asked, "Why didn't you leave? I mean, you had the keys."

Fonzo looked up at him and said, "I don't know how to drive."

Quietly and quickly, they set out for the task at hand. Ed gathered as many containers as he could find, and Fonzo started siphoning gas from as many cars as he could, filling up the containers. Once they completed that, Ed found some scraps of rope and started tying down the containers inside the bus. Then he fashioned some rags on top of each one. "Like a Molotov cocktail huh," Fonzo said.

"But, way more potent."

Once they had everything secured, Ed asked him, "You coming...or staying?"

Fonzo gazed around at the buildings. The neighborhood that he once considered home. The abandoned vehicles. Abandoned homes. Bodies that were left on the street. Some of them, people he knew. He thought about the destruction and horror that he'd witnessed firsthand and shook his head, turned towards Ed and asked him, "Where are you going?"

Ed also looked around, but not long before he answered, "To tell you the truth. Probably no place better than this. But, I'll say this. If there is a better place. You better damn sure believe I'm going to find it."

Then, Fonzo uttered, "Or, at least die trying."

Ed stared at him a moment, then said, "Well. Get your shit and let's get the fuck outta here."

"Where are we going?"

He thought about the piers. Manhattan. The Island. Going back. But he also thought about the destruction. And he asked himself the question. Was it worth it? Somberly, he answered, saying, "Somewhere better than here."

www.ingramcontent.com/pod-product-compliance
Lightning Source LLC
Chambersburg PA
CBHW071342130626
46556CB00005B/1988